SUPER DC HEROES

WONDER WOMAN

RUMBLE IN THE RAINFOREST

WRITTEN BY
SARAH HINES STEPHENS

ILLUSTRATED BY
DAN SCHOENING

WONDER WOMAN
CREATED BY
WILLIAM MOULTON MARSTON

STONE ARCH BOOKS
a capstone imprint

Published by Stone Arch Books in 2011
A Capstone Imprint
1710 Roe Crest Drive
North Mankato, Minnesota 56003
www.capstonepub.com

Cataloging-in-Publication Data is available on the Library of Congress
website.

ISBN: 978-1-4342-1992-3 (library binding)
ISBN: 978-1-4342-2765-2 (paperback)

Summary: While visiting the rainforest, Wonder Woman discovers that
a logging company has secretly destroyed a large area of trees. Traveling
deeper into the forest to investigate, she is suddenly attacked by two angry
villains — Poison Ivy and Gorilla Grodd! These foes soon realize that
they share a common enemy with the Amazon Princess. And, for one day,
they'll unite to stop the destruction of their habitat before it's lost forever.

Art Director: Bob Lentz
Designer: Kay Fraser
Production Specialist: Michelle Biedscheid

Printed in the United States of America in Stevens Point, Wisconsin.
012012
006569R

TABLE OF CONTENTS

CHAPTER 1

RAINFOREST AT RISK.......... 4

CHAPTER 2

PROTECTING THE HABITAT.......12

CHAPTER 3

TWO AGAINST ONE............ 24

CHAPTER 4

FRIENDLY ENEMIES............ 36

CHAPTER 5

DAWN OF A NEW DAY 44

RAINFOREST AT RISK

In the main ballroom of a hotel, men and women wearing nametags and fancy clothes chatted politely. It was the opening night of the Global Environmental Conference. Business people and politicians tried to enjoy a few social moments before the real work began.

Princess Diana, the ambassador of the island of Themyscira, smiled. She extended her hand to a bald man standing in front of her. "Pleasure to meet you, Mr. Javlar," she said.

The man shook her hand but didn't return the greeting. He looked past Diana and grumbled about the lack of air conditioning.

Diana wasn't fazed by his rudeness. She hadn't expected the rich businessman to be polite. She knew him by reputation only, but that reputation was hardly good. Rupert Javlar was known for going after profits without considering others. He cared about nothing but money and would sell his own mother to make a buck.

However, during the last year, Javlar appeared to have turned over a new leaf. According to news sources, he was now using his money for good. Javlar had reportedly done charity work in many developing areas of the world, including the conference's host country, Ryancar.

In fact, Ryancar's government had just given Javlar a large piece of rainforest. They had placed the businessman in charge of protecting the land. Any development was supposed to help the environment and the small nation.

"The Javlar Industries Water Treatment Plant is the greenest there is," said Javlar, bragging to anyone who would listen. "It's almost a miracle. We can turn seawater into drinking water."

Diana listened to every word. Her expression did not change, but she began to wonder. Why would a country with heavy rainfall and many rivers need a water treatment plant? The billionaire's change of heart and his interest in the tiny nation, rich with ancient hardwood, triggered Princess Diana's alarm bells.

For decades, Javlar had made his money mining diamonds and selling the treasures of poor nations. What, if anything, would make him stop taking and start giving?

Certainly, recent environmental laws had made Javlar's huge profits harder to come by. But when Diana looked into the billionaire's face, she suspected that his latest project was not the "gift" to Ryancar that he claimed. There had to be something in it for him.

A woman with a notebook stepped closer to Javlar. She waited politely for Javlar to stop talking about the wonderful "favor" he was doing for Ryancar. Then she asked a few questions of her own. According to her sources, new reports of polluted water, smoke, and noise surrounding his plant were coming in all of the time.

"What's your reaction to these reports, Mr. Javlar?" Diana asked.

Javlar tried to return the smile. He parted his lips but only managed to bare his teeth. "Everything I am doing to help Ryancar is perfectly legal," he said, struggling to remain calm. "I was granted that land and everything on it to do as I see fit. It is mine fair and square. I own it, and we are making progress." He glanced around the room again and scowled at the open window. "Could somebody shut that?" he snapped. "The fresh air is making me sick."

Diana stepped closer to the warm breeze blowing in from outside. Listening to Javlar was making *her* feel a little sick. She knew something was not right, but she hadn't completely figured it out yet.

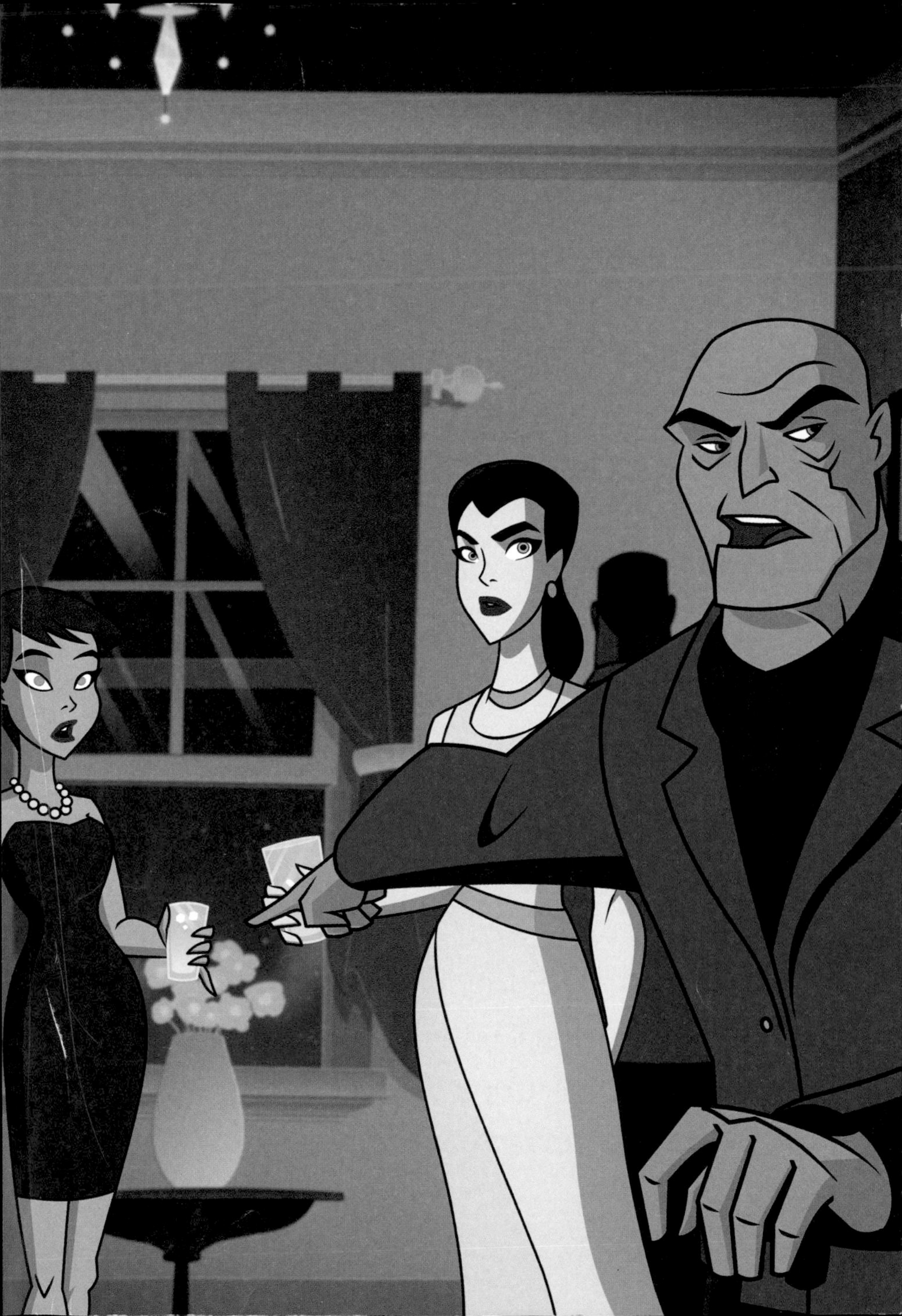

The princess took a deep breath and studied the bubbles dancing in her glass of sparkling water. The tiny orbs reminded her of fish in a sea or stars in the sky. She wondered how a person could feel they owned a piece of land and everything on it. *How does one "own" a tree? What about the animals that made it a home, the oxygen it produced, the carbon dioxide it cleaned from the air? Could a person "own" all of that?* Diana wondered.

"Nobody wants to talk about the good things I'm doing!" Javlar complained. "The water treatment plant will allow this nation to develop. Javlar is paving the way. You will see!"

A tour of Javlar's plant was scheduled for the morning. All of the conference members were invited, including Diana.

Diana could not wait that long. As she
made her way out of the crowded room,
she was haunted by memories of her
own island home. Themyscira was lush
and green like Ryancar. The thought of
someone poisoning its air and water made
her shudder. It was something her Amazon
sisters would never allow to happen there.
It was something she could not allow to
happen here.

Out of sight of conference goers, Diana
began to spin.

When she twirled to a stop, Diana was
dressed in a red, white, and blue warrior
uniform. She was Wonder Woman, and she
was ready to take action.

CHAPTER 2

PROTECTING THE HABITAT

Entering the forest, Wonder Woman felt instantly at home. She found the sounds of the rainforest creatures comforting as she made her way toward Javlar's plant.

Though she could have flown, Wonder Woman enjoyed running through the trees. She leaped over logs and ran easily through the thick vegetation. The closer she got to Javlar's land, the more signs she began to see that all was not well. Smoke choked the air. A few feet later, a barbed wire fence with a metal sign read, "Hazard Area."

"'Hazard' might be putting it mildly," Wonder Woman said. Leaping over the wire, she pushed farther into the rainforest. Suddenly, she found herself on the edge of a clearing.

CLANK! BANG! BZZZT!

Noisy machines, smoke, and the smell of gasoline were everywhere. Taking cover behind a tree trunk, she peered out at the situation. What she saw tied her stomach in knots.

Machines equipped with saw blades and limb strippers were working all over the rainforest. Even in the dim light, Wonder Woman could tell the machines were not being run by humans. These robots were remote-controlled, designed to destroy the forest on their own, under the cover of darkness.

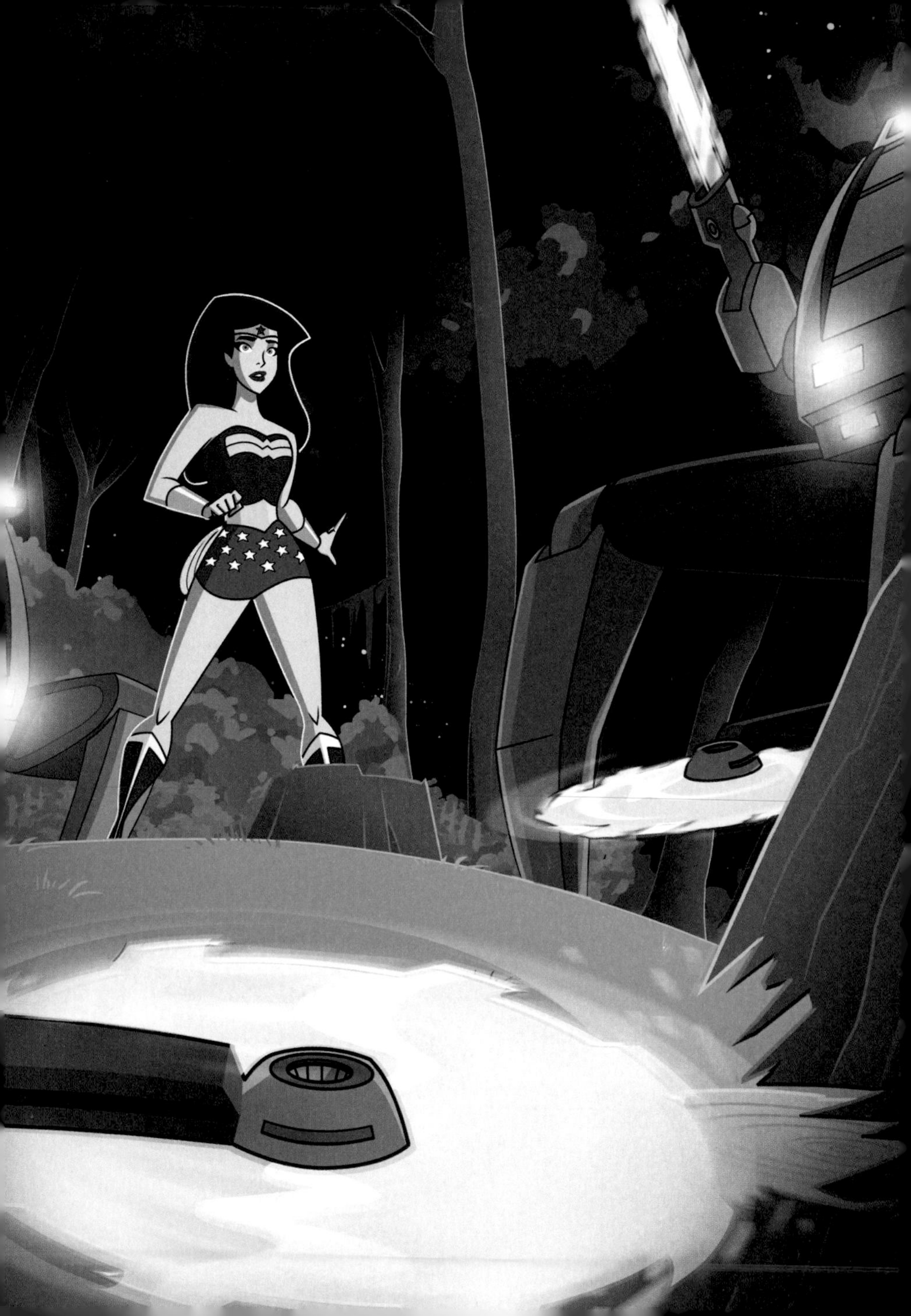

Like mechanical insects, the robots crawled over the landscape doing the work of their master. In minutes, they were able to chop down a tree and strip the branches. Then the machines tied three logs together and launched them down the river.

When the robots were done cutting trees, they set fire to all that remained. Flames smoldered around the edge of the clearing. The resulting mud and ash drained into the river, poisoning it. When the robots were done, there was nothing left.

Sensing her sadness, a lonely gibbon crept onto Wonder Woman's shoulder and shivered by her ear. Wonder Woman reached up to stroke its fur. She made soothing sounds, understanding that the creature had lost its home to these robots.

The gibbon was only one of many animals that had lost their home. And for what? Wonder Woman was certain she knew the answer to that question already. What she needed was proof that Javlar was behind this crime. She needed a piece of equipment with his name on it.

While Wonder Woman thought how to get it, three logs were lashed, launched, and beginning their float downstream. The Amazon Princess made her way closer. Downstream was where she would find her proof. She was about to climb aboard a raft when something shook the ground.

The sound of tree branches snapping like twigs echoed in the night. It was coming from the woods behind her.

Leaping into a nearby tree, Wonder Woman strained her eyes to get a look. Even with her amazing powers, Wonder Woman could tell only one thing — the object was closing in fast!

Throughout the forest, animals scurried to get out of the way. Branches whipped back and forth. Wonder Woman put her hand on the gibbon on her shoulder. The animal shivered and dashed away to seek cover. Alone in the dark, Wonder Woman waited for whatever it was to show itself.

It would have been a surprise to see another of Rupert Javlar's machines come hurtling out of the trees. However, what emerged into the clearing was even more shocking. It was Gorilla Grodd!

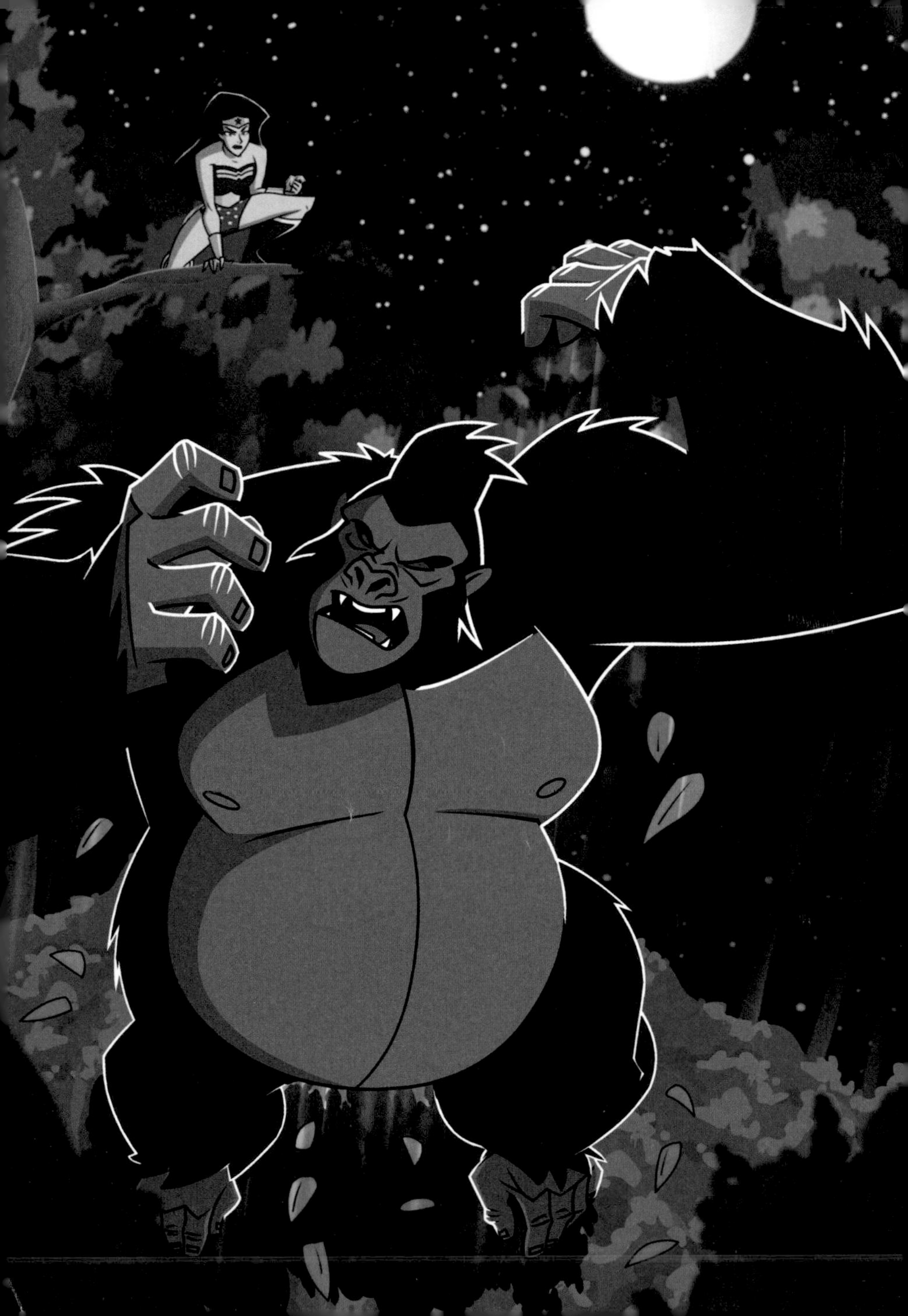

The black-furred villain burst out of the jungle, moving so fast Wonder Woman hardly recognized him. She could not recall when she had last seen the giant gorilla, but she knew it had not been a happy moment. Grodd was smart and powerful. He was known to be a member of the Secret Society of Super-Villains, a gang of the world's worst criminals. The ape had visions of one day ruling the planet. What he was doing here was a mystery, but Wonder Woman knew he wasn't happy.

Grodd stood and let out a scream.

Unafraid of the robots working all around him, Grodd used his telekinetic powers to pick up a tree. He spun the trunk with his mind and sent it swinging.

That's when Wonder Woman spotted another surprise. Riding on Grodd's back, and sending snaky green tendrils around his throat, was Poison Ivy! She was the evil alter ego of botanist Pamela Isley. Through experiments with plants, Isley had become a toxic super-villain and would stop at nothing to protect her vegetative kin.

Thankfully, the villains were so locked in battle they did not notice Wonder Woman.

With a screech, Ivy pulled Grodd's hair. She jumped from his back and landed directly in front of him. Then she blew poison pollen from her hand into his face.

Grodd showed each of his giant teeth. He covered his face with his furry hands and stumbled back, blinded. When he took his hands away, he was angrier than ever.

The gorilla's curled fist was the size of a beach ball. He brought it down on the spot where Ivy had been rooted last.

 Too late. She was gone!

As the effects of the pollen faded, Grodd blinked his eyes and peered around into the dark. While searching for something to throw at Ivy, he saw the destroyed patch of forest for the first time. He blinked rapidly in the direction of a line of motionless robots. Suddenly, the mass of metal roared to life.

Grodd looked down the line. Then he swung his paw and knocked a machine that sprayed a sticky, flammable liquid straight toward Ivy. Poison Ivy laughed at her attacker. Two could play at that game.

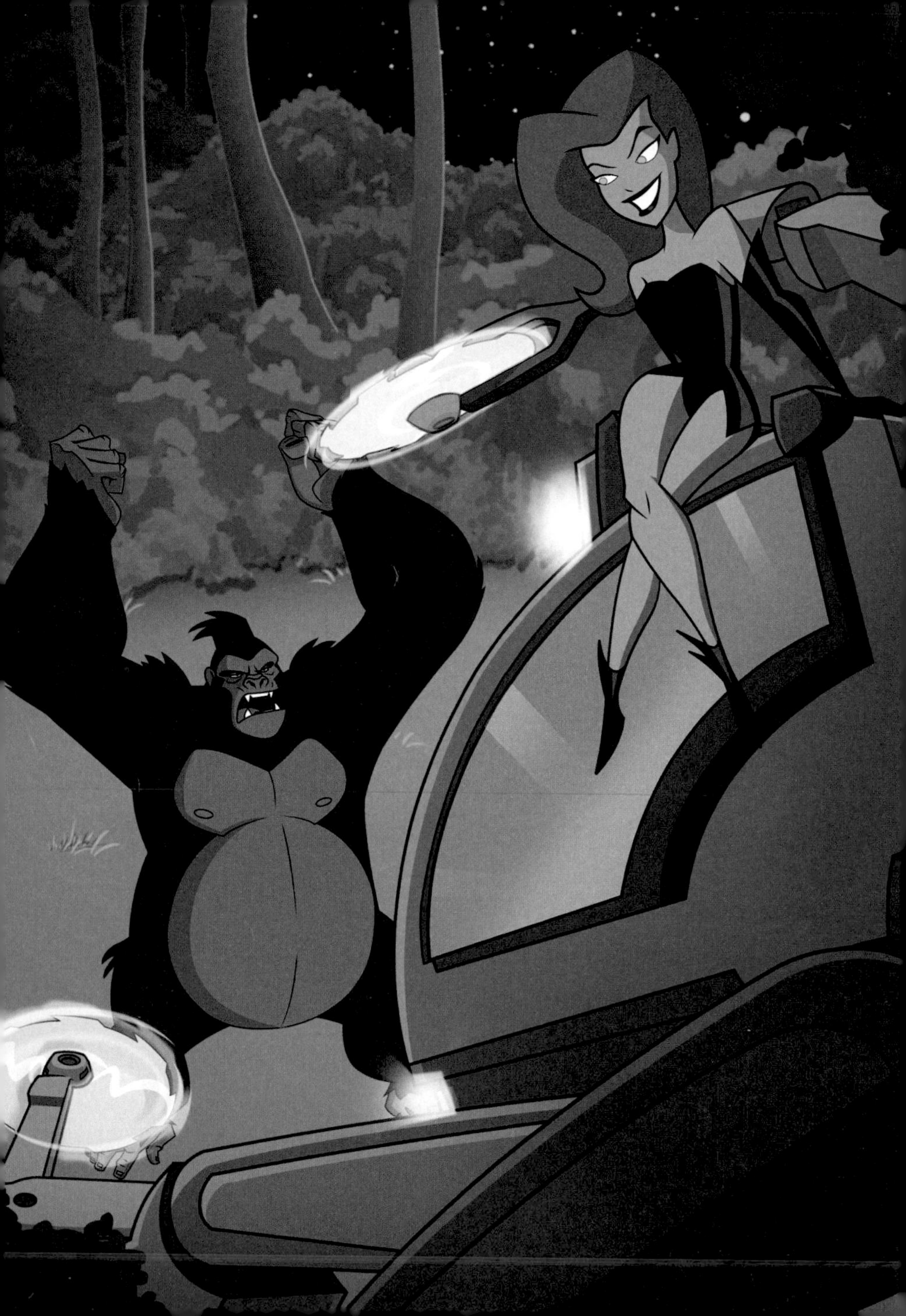

Using a vine, she swung to the top of another machine. Commanding an army of roots and leaves to do her dirty work, Ivy steered toward Grodd.

Wonder Woman braced for the impact, but it never came. Before the machines could clash, Wonder Woman sneezed loudly — she was allergic to Poison Ivy.

Somehow, the sudden noise broke Grodd's concentration, and Ivy turned to look. The machines rolled to a stop, and Wonder Woman jumped from her hiding place into the clearing.

"Hello," she greeted them both.

Having been beaten by Wonder Woman in the past, neither Grodd nor Ivy had any love for the Amazon warrior. What they did have was a new, and common, enemy.

CHAPTER 3

TWO AGAINST ONE

Within seconds, Poison Ivy and Gorilla Grodd had teamed up to defeat Wonder Woman. Using all of their powers, they sent two saws wheeling toward the super hero.

CHING! CHING!

Wonder Woman deflected the buzzing blades of the first robot with the shiny cuffs on her wrists. The silver bracelets crumpled the steel blades like foil. The first robot ground to a halt, and Wonder Woman whirled to face the next machine.

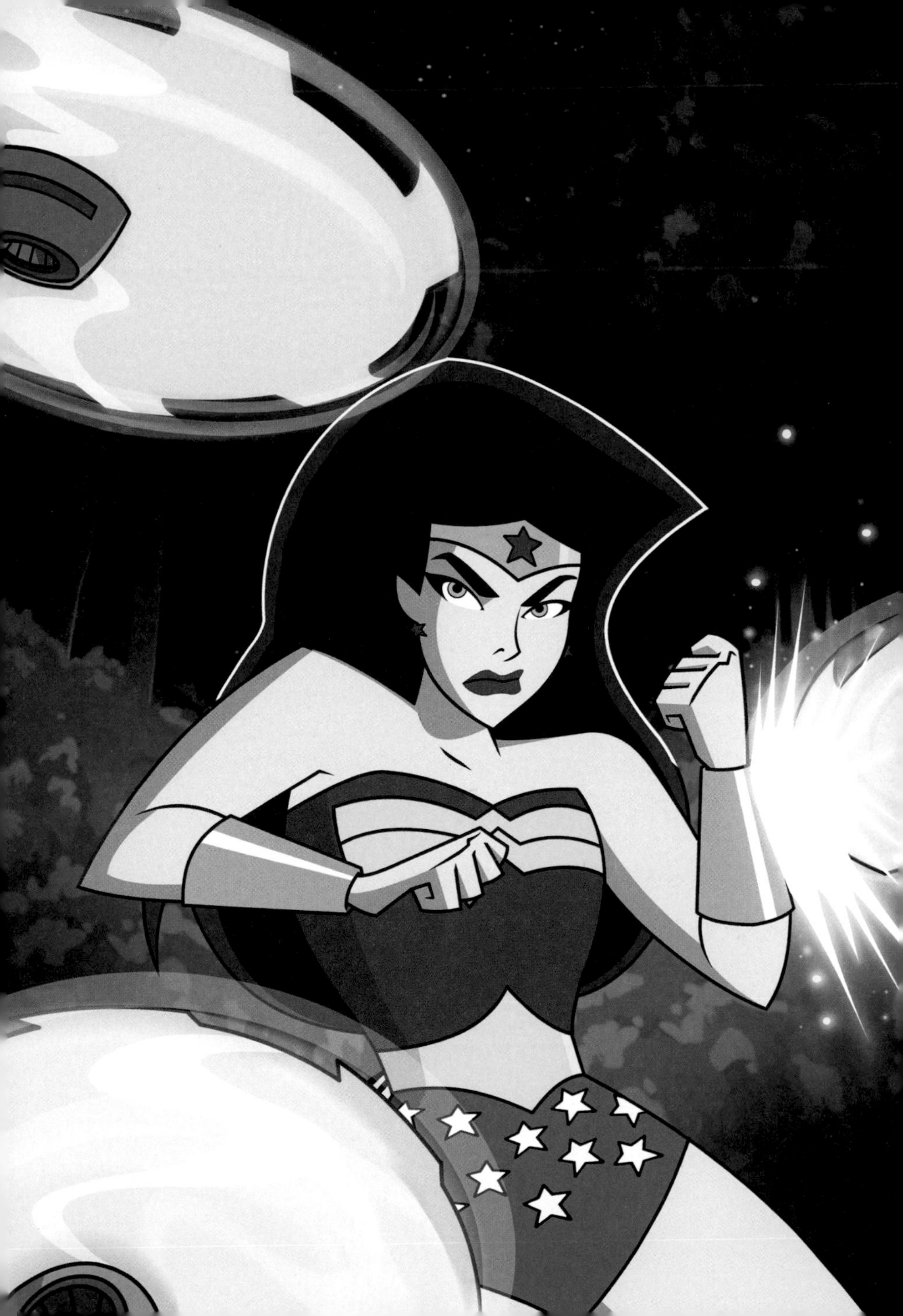

Whipping off her tiara, Wonder Woman threw the golden band. With the flick of her wrist, she sent it sailing toward the operator's seat. It circled the controls and shut down the blade.

The machines fell silent. Grodd and Ivy stared at Wonder Woman with narrowed eyes. She could almost feel them planning their next move. In that instant, Wonder Woman knew what she had to do. She turned and ran.

"Coward!" Grodd growled. He came after her with Ivy on his heels. Wonder Woman jumped onto one of the log floats and stood waiting with her hands on her hips.

Grodd jumped after her. **THUD!** He landed chest-first on the wooden raft, making it rock and shake. Ivy was next, landing gracefully behind Grodd.

Wonder Woman tightened her grasp on the rope coiled at her side. Her foes were right where she wanted them. She twirled her lasso in the air once and then let it wrap around them both. The villains were caught, snared together in Wonder Woman's Lasso of Truth. All three of them were headed downstream.

"We have to talk," Wonder Woman said calmly. "I'll go first."

"So speak!" Grodd said, snarling. His giant gorilla chest heaved under Wonder Woman's Golden Lasso. His curled lips showed huge yellow fangs.

Wonder Woman didn't flinch. Making a villain see reason was never an easy task. Luckily, it was one that Wonder Woman, gifted with compassion and skilled in mind control, was well suited for.

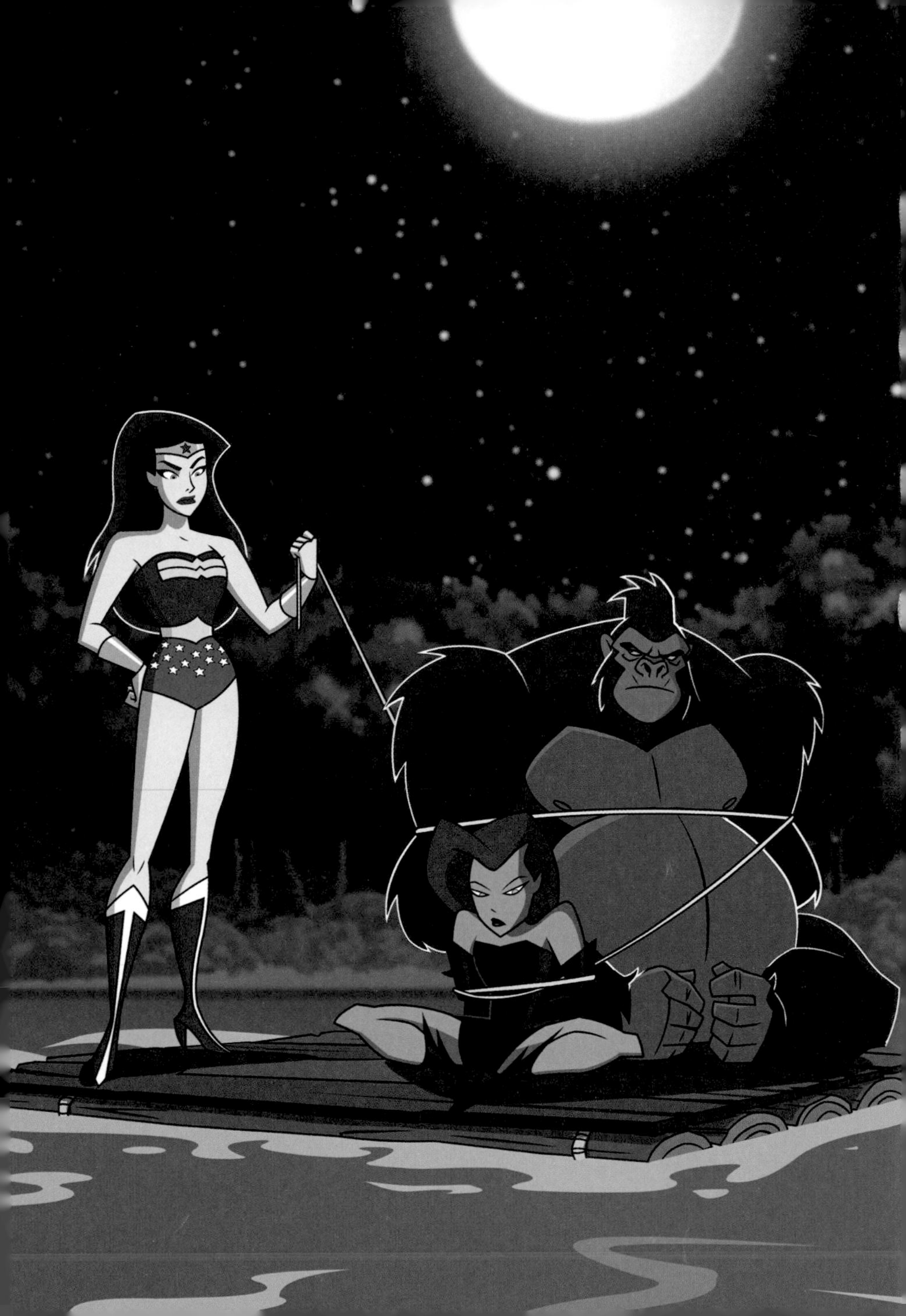

Wonder Woman tapped into her foes' minds and quickly understood why Poison Ivy and Gorilla Grodd were here. Both of them, strange as it was, had come to Ryancar for the same reason — to stop the rainforest from being destroyed.

Grodd believed that humans were weaker than animals. He did not want to see wildlife habitats destroyed. In his mind, the destruction of nature for profit was proof that people were simple creatures. He viewed the loss of animal life as wasting armies he would one day need to gain control of the planet.

Poison Ivy had similar feelings about vegetation. Being part plant herself, she could control almost anything green. She was able to make plants do her evil bidding, but only if they were alive.

A small smile crept onto Wonder Woman's face as they floated closer to a small mountain. A plan was coming together in her head. Capturing both of the villains was, in fact, a gift. If she could convince them to work together, she would have two very powerful allies.

The raft of logs sailed into the side of a mountain, cutting off the last of the light. "You realize, of course, why we are here?" Wonder Woman asked her captives.

"We?" asked Ivy. She hated the idea of being stuck in the same group as these stinkweeds. "I am here for my leafy friends," she shouted.

"Yes, the plant life," Wonder Woman said. "It's terrible what Javlar is doing to the jungle. After all, it provides home and food to the animals, right Grodd?"

ROOAAARRR!! Grodd couldn't stand when humans were right. "I thought you were the one driving the animals out," he admitted to Ivy.

"What do I care about things with fur and feathers?" Ivy looked disgusted at the thought. She rustled her leaves. "When I found you thrashing around the forest, I thought you were the problem," she said.

ROOAAARRR!! Grodd roared again.

"He's not," Wonder Woman said. Slowly, she began to unwind her lasso. "And neither am I, but I know who is."

At that moment, the raft entered a giant cavern within the mountain. If Wonder Woman's hunch was right, they were at the back entrance of Javlar's water treatment plant — the cover for his logging operation.

The logs they were riding were pulled to the side by two robots. Wonder Woman hopped off and untied her captives. They followed the Amazon Princess to the far side of the cavern. Nobody spoke. Robots worked all around them, taking trees out of the water, treating, and stacking the illegal hardwoods.

Ivy shook her head and turned away in disgust when she saw the drying wood. Javlar had destroyed hundreds of trees that had taken thousands of years to grow.

"Javlar's water plant is a cover to ship lumber without government permission," Wonder Woman explained. "He needed land close to a river and near the ocean so he could get the wood to the market. By day, he may be treating water, but at night this place is a funeral home for the forest."

The super hero pointed out the river highway they'd ridden in on flowing out the other side of the cave. The mighty Amazon Princess finished by stating her case. "We can stop him," she said, "if we work together."

Slowly, Gorilla Grodd nodded his huge head. Poison Ivy hesitated, staring at them both with her green eyes. Then she nodded, too. But before the three could all shake hands, they were interrupted by a new sound.

The sound of metal scraping against solid rock sent a chill up Wonder Woman's spine. **SKREEEEEEEECH!**

Heavy footsteps echoed, and a massive robot lurched into view.

The metal man was almost two stories tall. It barely fit inside the giant cavern. His hands were spinning blades. From far below, Wonder Woman saw a human figure behind the robot's glass-bubble head. This robot was not like the others. A person onboard was commanding it.

HAHAHAHA!

The irritating laugh that echoed from giant speakers left no doubt. Rupert Javlar was at the controls!

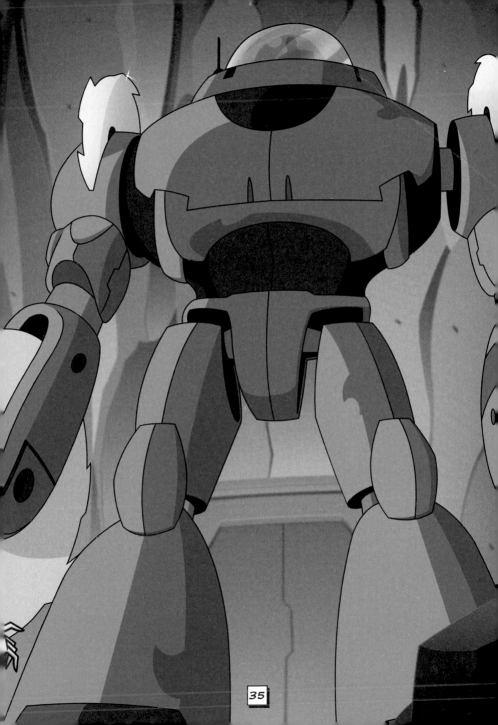

CHAPTER 4

FRIENDLY ENEMIES

"That's him," Wonder Woman said. Her eyes were fixed on the man inside the machine. Poison Ivy and Gorilla Grodd understood. Rupert Javlar was the person responsible for the destruction of the rainforest on Ryancar. He was the man they were all looking for. He was their new enemy, and he was commanding the two-story robot.

Unfortunately, the machine Javlar was inside of looked nearly indestructible, and he was not about to let them in.

Javlar pushed a button on the control panel. **BZZZT!** With a buzz of gears, the robot's blades were replaced by mighty pincers. Javlar gripped and ungripped the metal blades, and then used them to pick up a giant pallet of machine parts. He held the tower of tools high over the heads of Wonder Woman, Grodd, and Ivy.

"Run!" Wonder Woman said. The three scattered. **WHAM!** The pallet crashed down, shooting steel in every direction.

Using his telekinetic powers, Grodd sent the tools back at Javlar. They bounced off the robot without leaving a dent.

Grodd looked around for something else. A grinding machine caught his attention, and he hurled it at the robot. **SMASH!**

Javlar's robot was still coming.

The powerful pincers at the end of each arm disappeared. This time flamethrowers emerged in their place. Flames dripped from them like saliva from the mouth of a drooling attack dog.

"Get behind the lumber. It's worth too much for him to burn!" Wonder Woman shouted to the others.

Ivy slunk behind the stacks of valuable wood. Grodd grunted and slapped his muscled chest. He hid from no one. Though he was only as tall as the robot's foot, he attacked the mechanical monster.

"Out of my way, monkey!" Javlar said.

Grodd's heavy brows slid farther down his dark face. He charged, grasped the robot's leg, and started to climb.

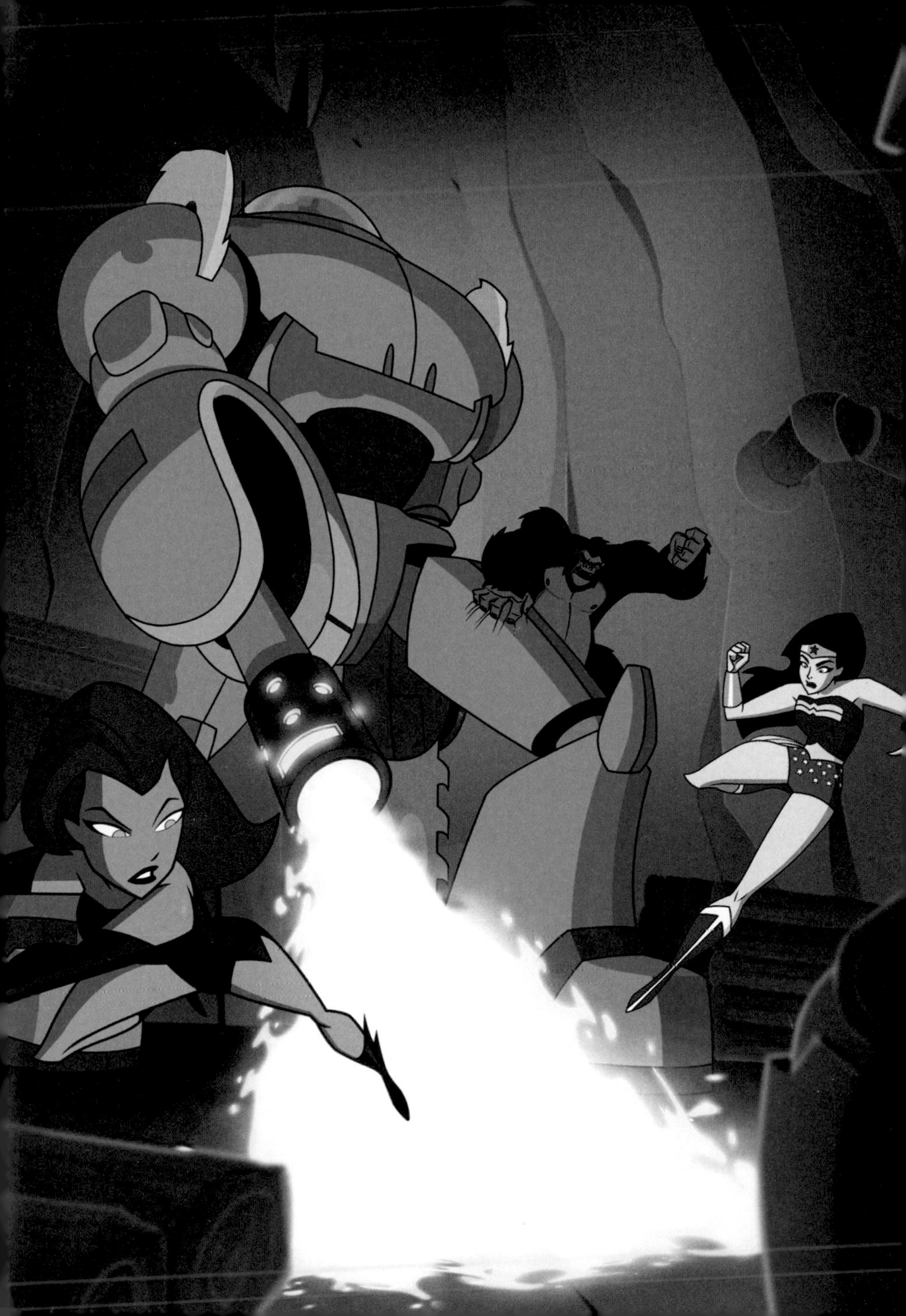

Javlar swung the robot's arms at Grodd. It was a weak effort, and the moment Wonder Woman had been waiting for.

She nodded to Ivy. While Grodd took care of Javlar, the two women had a clear shot. Wonder Woman smelled a flowery scent and at the same time knew what Ivy had in mind. Ivy was using plant smells to communicate, and it confirmed that they were thinking the same thing.

While Grodd pounded on the robot's outer shell, Wonder Woman and Ivy moved in. She flipped her lasso, using it like a whip to snare one of the robot's arms. The machine let loose a burst of flames. Javlar struggled to fight off Grodd and Wonder Woman one-handed. Then Ivy snagged his other arm in a mass of vines.

The rope-like plants twined their way around the metal quickly. Then Wonder Woman and Poison Ivy bound both arms to the robot's chest.

"That should hold him," said Wonder Woman.

Inside the clear head of the robot, Javlar punched at the controls. He could not aim his weapons. His laughter turned to angry shouts as he realized the fight was over. He had lost. But Grodd was not finished.

The gorilla stood on a stack of lumber and began destroying the millionaire's machinery with his own equipment. Robots flew threw the air. Each one found its mark.

When Grodd was finished, Javlar and his machines looked like a pile of scraps.

Only the glass dome, with Javlar inside, was visible at the top of the twisted metal pile. Javlar stabbed at the button to open his hatch. Nothing happened. He was trapped — a prisoner in his own creation.

"Just wait!" he shouted through the bulletproof casing.

Wonder Woman could not hold back a slight smile. She was excited to see the faces of everyone attending the environmental conference when they came for their tour of Javlar's "gift" to Ryancar. They would get a big surprise. It would be hard to remain patient, but the wait would be worth it.

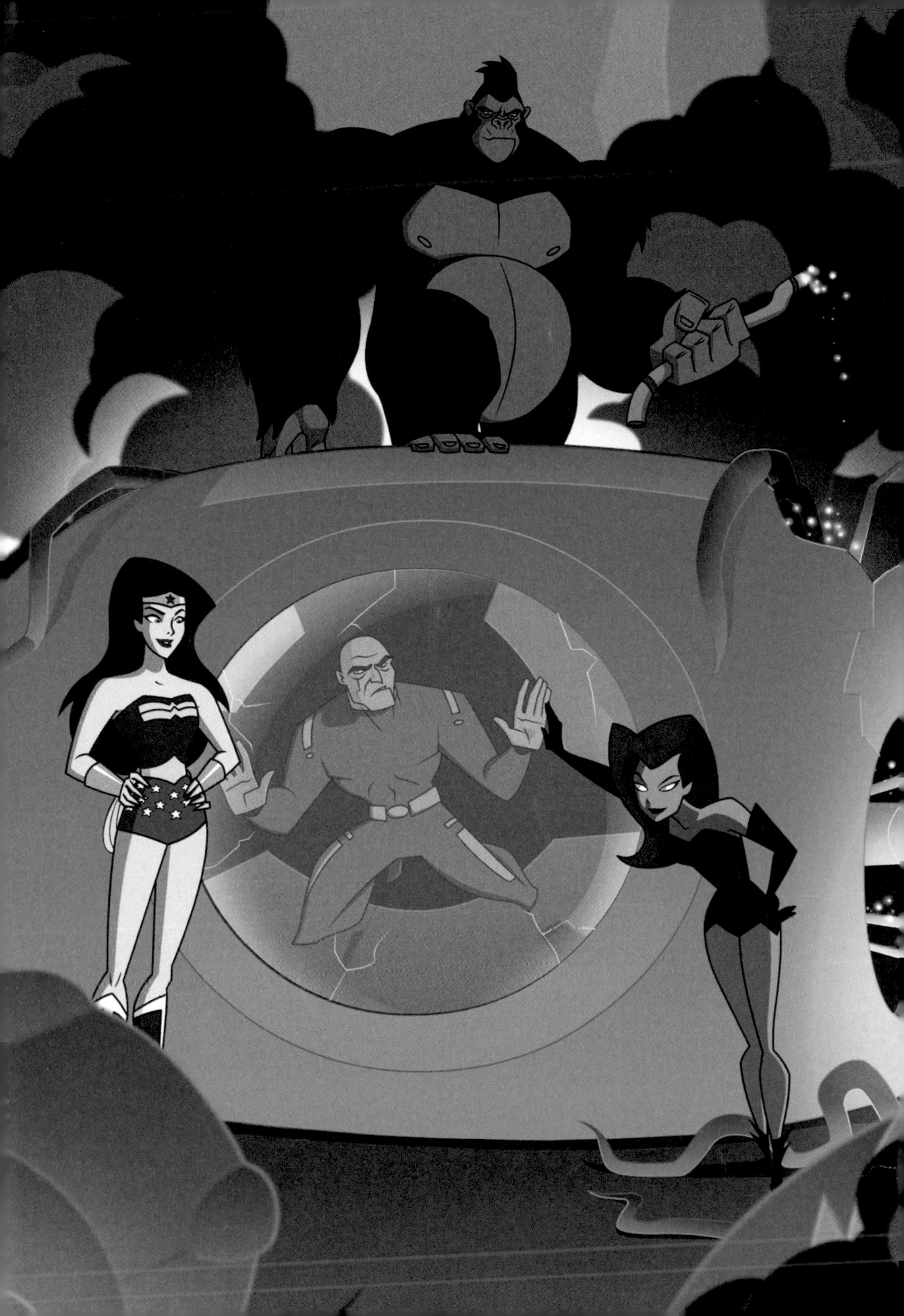

DAWN OF A NEW DAY

When the conference attendees arrived, Princess Diana was already waiting. She stood with several reporters, photographers, and six members of the Ryancar police department.

"Right this way," the princess said.

Diana rushed the officers past the tanks and pools, up the river, all the way to the back of the plant. On the way, she pointed out the running water. "Isn't it odd that the river is so filled with mud and ash?" she questioned.

When the group stepped inside the giant cave on the far side of the plant, it took a moment for most people's eyes to adjust. However, Princess Diana saw what was right in front of her, just as she had from the beginning.

"As you can see, Javlar has made great strides in . . . padding his bank accounts by selling off Ryancar's forest," said the princess.

There were several gasps from the crowd as they took in the situation. Rupert Javlar was still trapped inside his robot suit. He was trapped in front of the racks of priceless hardwood he had stolen from the rainforest.

Grodd and Ivy were nowhere to be seen. Only Diana noticed Ivy's green tendrils growing out of the nearby tunnel.

Then Diana heard a snort that had to be Grodd, laughing at the downfall of a human enemy. The villains stayed hidden in the dark, as they had agreed, to watch Javlar's arrest.

It had taken some doing to convince Grodd not to crush Javlar after they'd captured him. Wonder Woman prevailed in the end by explaining that justice could only be served if Javlar was alive to face trial. He would be forced to spend all of his profits to help fix the damage.

In a way, Javlar would serve as an example. His crimes could be enough to anger the conference attendees and many others who only read about the destruction of Ryancar. It might even cause other people to do something to protect the environment.

If everyone did something, they could make a real difference. That is what Princess Diana told the crowd, ending her speech by pointing to Javlar's junk heap. "I think Rupert Javlar is ready for recycling," she announced. Her voice was lost in the applause that continued as the police pried off the robot's lid and put Javlar in handcuffs.

The conference attendees clapped again as Javlar was led out of the room. It was clear that a step had been taken to turn the tide of destruction and begin the work of protecting the earth's environment. They were ready for more.

Princess Diana was the last to leave to cavern. She glanced back at the dark tunnel where her unexpected allies were hiding and smiled to herself.

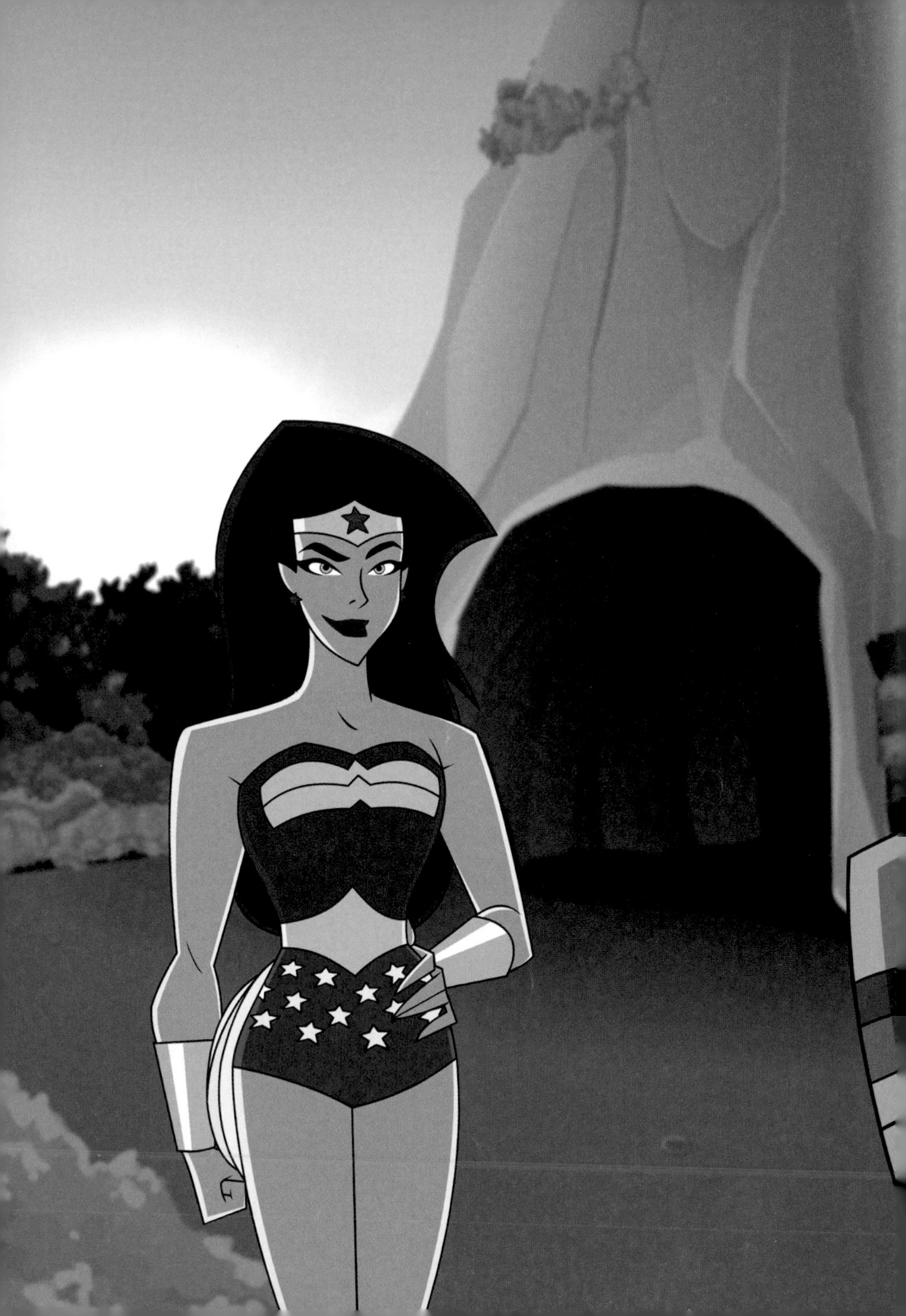

Never would she have imagined teaming up with sworn enemies, but they had come together for the sake of the planet, and so could the nations' leaders. Wonder Woman was sure of it.

INVISIBLE PLANE
SECRET FILES

FILE NO. 3765 >>> GORILLA GRODD

ENEMY » | ALLY | FRIEND

BASE: Gorilla City, Africa

OCCUPATION: World Conqueror

HEIGHT: 6' 6" **WEIGHT:** 600 lbs

EYES: Gray **HAIR:** Black

POWERS/ABILITIES: Ingenious scientist and inventor; can control others and transform matter with "Force of Mind" power; ability to transfer his mind into other bodies.

BIOGRAPHY

A race of super-intelligent apes exists in the deepest jungle of Africa. Known as Gorilla City, the kingdom is ruled by King Solovar, a kind and noble ape. Unfortunately, one unruly member, Gorilla Grodd, has other plans for the highly evolved primates. He wants to conquer the humans and rule Earth, once and for all. Although others refuse to follow, Grodd promises to continue his evil pursuits alone.

FORCE OF MIND

Powerful mind-control skills make Grodd's brain his deadliest weapon:

Telepathy (tuh-LEH-puh-thee) — the ability to communicate using the mind alone. Grodd is capable of speaking to other animals and humans simply by thinking. He can also gain secret information by reading the minds of others.

Telekinesis (teh-lih-ki-NEE-sis) — the ability to move objects from one place to another without touching them. Using only his mind, Gorilla Grodd can hurl even the heaviest objects at his enemies. He can also transform matter, twisting metal or crushing boulders into dust.

WEAKNESSES

Although Gorilla Grodd is hard to stop, the Amazon Princess has several options for defeating the evil ape:

1. The Golden Lasso of Truth is potentially the most effective weapon against this super-intelligent animal. Although Grodd's brain can be deadly, the Golden Lasso's mind-controlling powers are unmatched.

2. Wonder Woman's animal instincts give her a unique advantage against this brilliant beast. The ability to track and communicate with animals allows the Amazon Princess to better understand her competitor.

3. Although the power of flight may seem useless against Gorilla Grodd, following the evil ape into the treetops is a necessary ability.

BIOGRAPHIES

Sarah Hines Stephens has authored more than 60 books for children and written about all kinds of characters, from Jedi to princesses. Though she has some stellar red boots, she is still holding out for an Invisible Jet and thinks a Lasso of Truth could come in handy parenting her two wonder kids. When she is not writing, gardening, or saving the world by teaching about recycling, Sarah enjoys spending time with her heroic husband and super friends.

Dan Schoening was born in Victoria, B.C. Canada. From an early age, Dan has had a passion for animation and comic books. Currently, Dan does freelance work in the animation and game industry and spends a lot of time with his lovely little daughter, Paige.

GLOSSARY

ambassador (am-BASS-uh-dur)—the top person sent by a government to represent it in another country or land

conference (KON-fur-uhnss)—a formal meeting for discussing ideas or opinions

habitat (HAB-uh-tat)—the place and natural conditions in which an animal lives

polluted (puh-LOO-tuhd)—contaminated or made dirty or impure

rainforest (RAYN-for-ist)—a dense, tropical jungle where a lot of rain falls

reputation (rep-yuh-TAY-shuhn)—your worth, or character, as judged by other people

tiara (tee-ER-uh)—a small crown; Wonder Woman can use her tiara as a weapon

toxic (TOK-sik)—poisonous

vegetation (vej-uh-TAY-shuhn)—plant life or the plants that cover an area

DISCUSSION QUESTIONS

1. Wonder Woman joined forces with two of her enemies to take down Rupert Javlar. Do you think she will remain friends with Gorilla Grodd and Poison Ivy? Why or why not?

2. The Amazon Princess used her superpowers to save part of the rainforest. What can you do to help the environment?

WRITING PROMPTS

1. Rupert Javlar destroyed part of the rainforest. How do you think he should be punished? Write a plan that would teach him a lesson.

2. Wonder Woman has many superpowers. If you could choose only one superpower, what would it be? Would you want to fly, run fast, or have X-ray vision? Write about your choice.

3. Write down at least one thing that you already do to help save the planet. Then describe two more things you will do in the future.

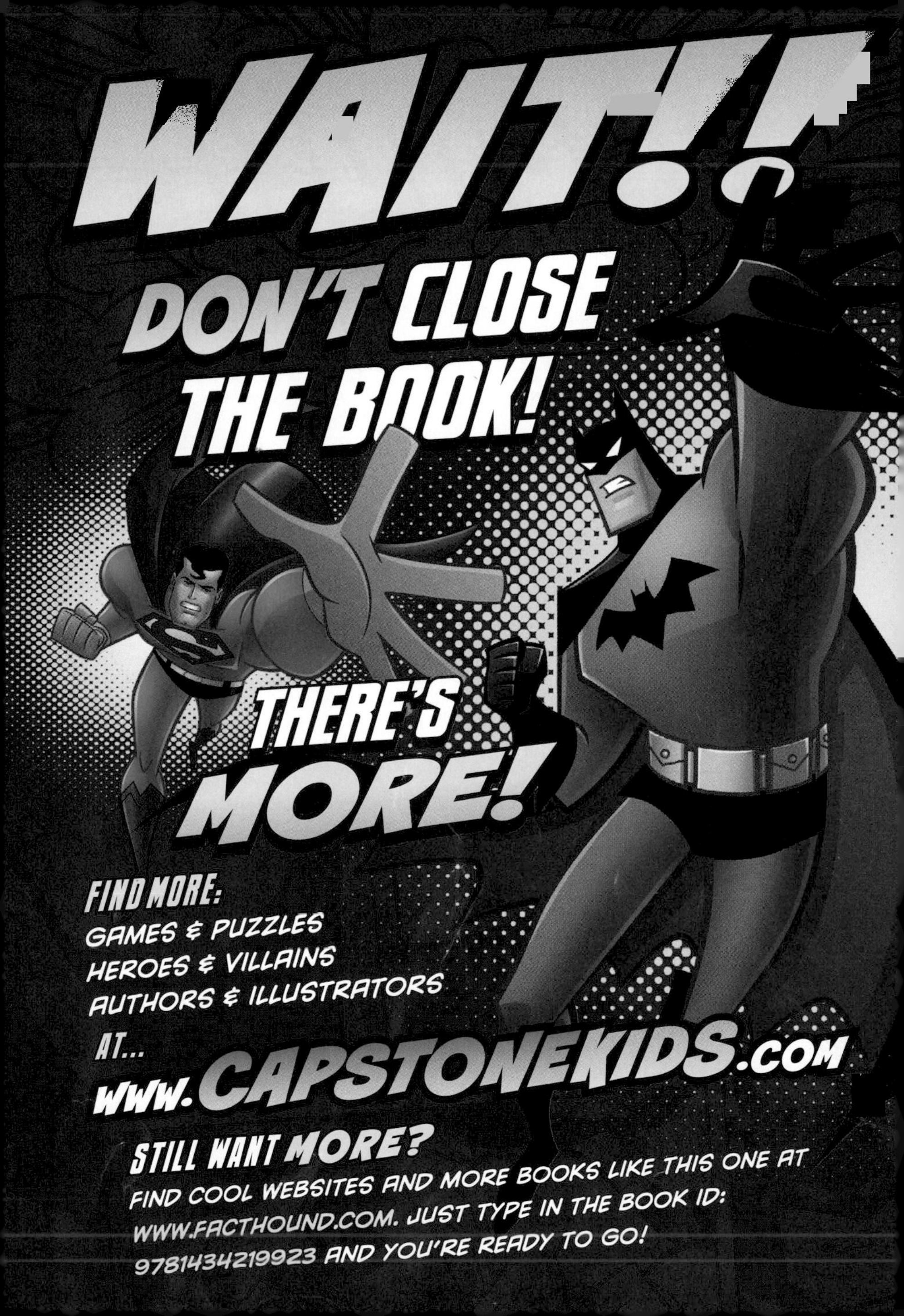
WAIT!!
DON'T CLOSE THE BOOK!
THERE'S MORE!
FIND MORE:
GAMES & PUZZLES
HEROES & VILLAINS
AUTHORS & ILLUSTRATORS
AT...
WWW.CAPSTONEKIDS.COM
STILL WANT MORE?
FIND COOL WEBSITES AND MORE BOOKS LIKE THIS ONE AT
WWW.FACTHOUND.COM. JUST TYPE IN THE BOOK ID:
9781434219923 AND YOU'RE READY TO GO!

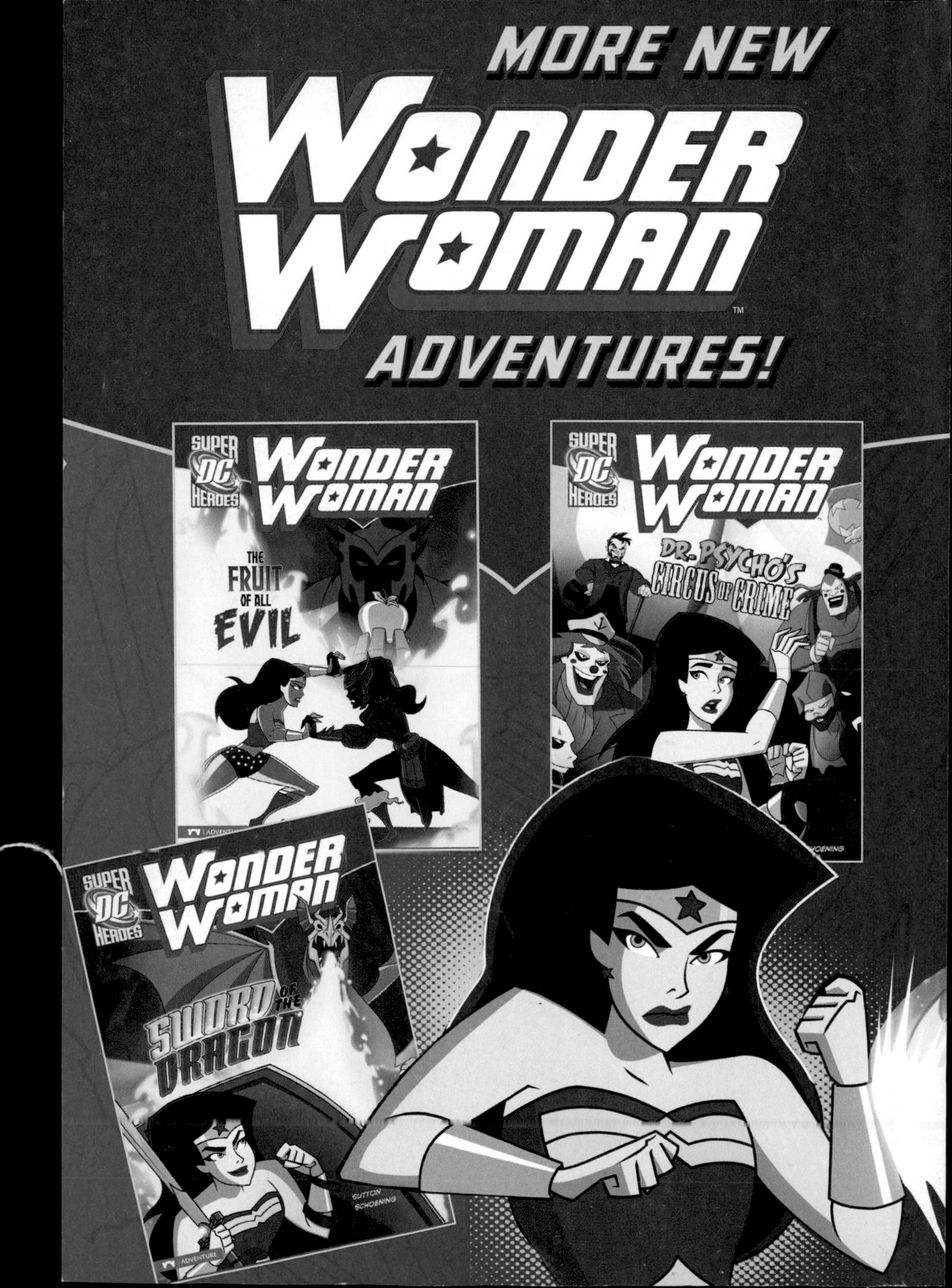
MORE NEW
WONDER WOMAN™
ADVENTURES!
SUPER DC HEROES
WONDER WOMAN
THE FRUIT OF ALL EVIL
SUPER DC HEROES
WONDER WOMAN
DR. PSYCHO'S CIRCUS OF CRIME
SUPER DC HEROES
WONDER WOMAN
SWORD OF THE DRAGON
SUTTON
SCHOENING
ADVENTURE

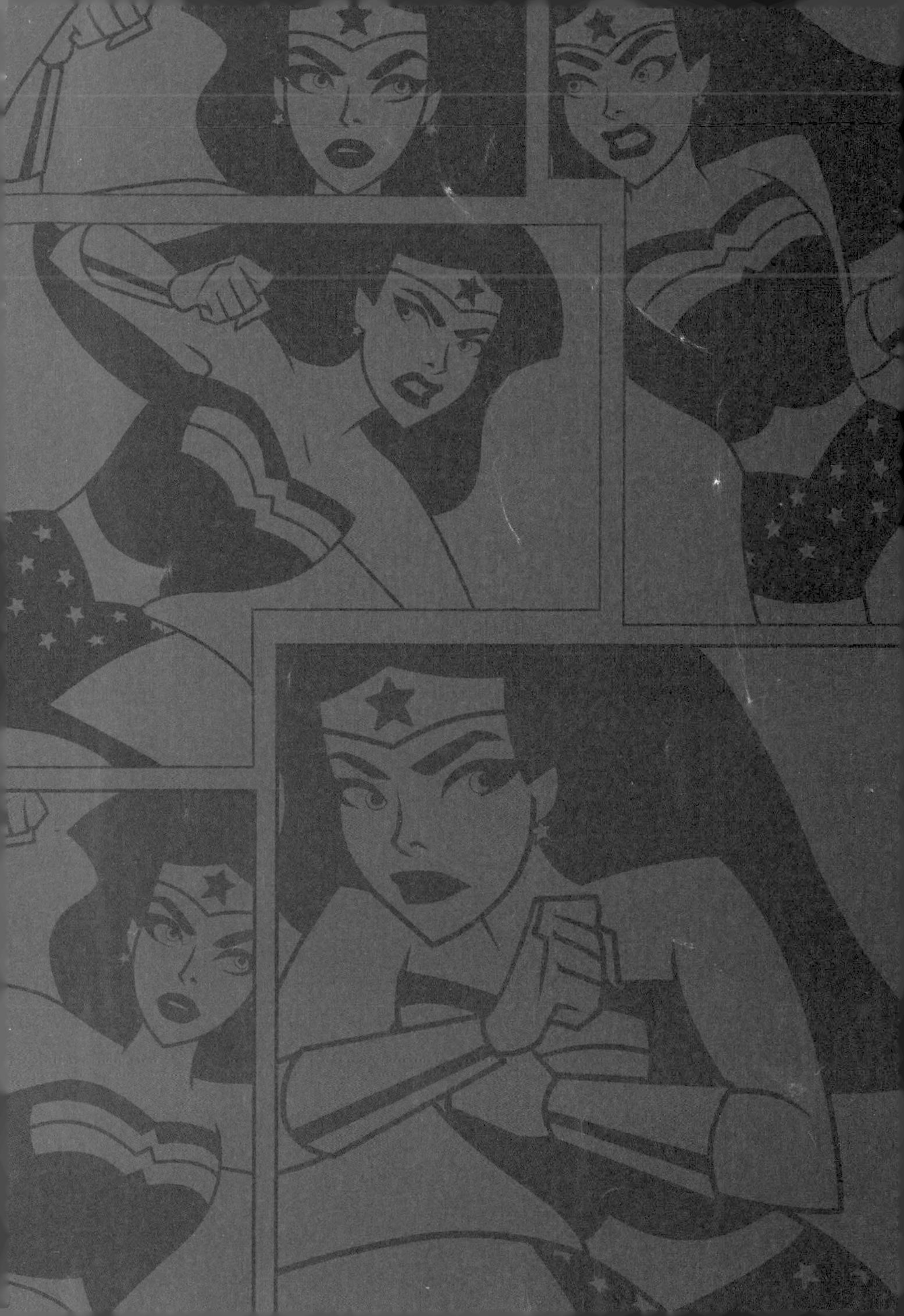

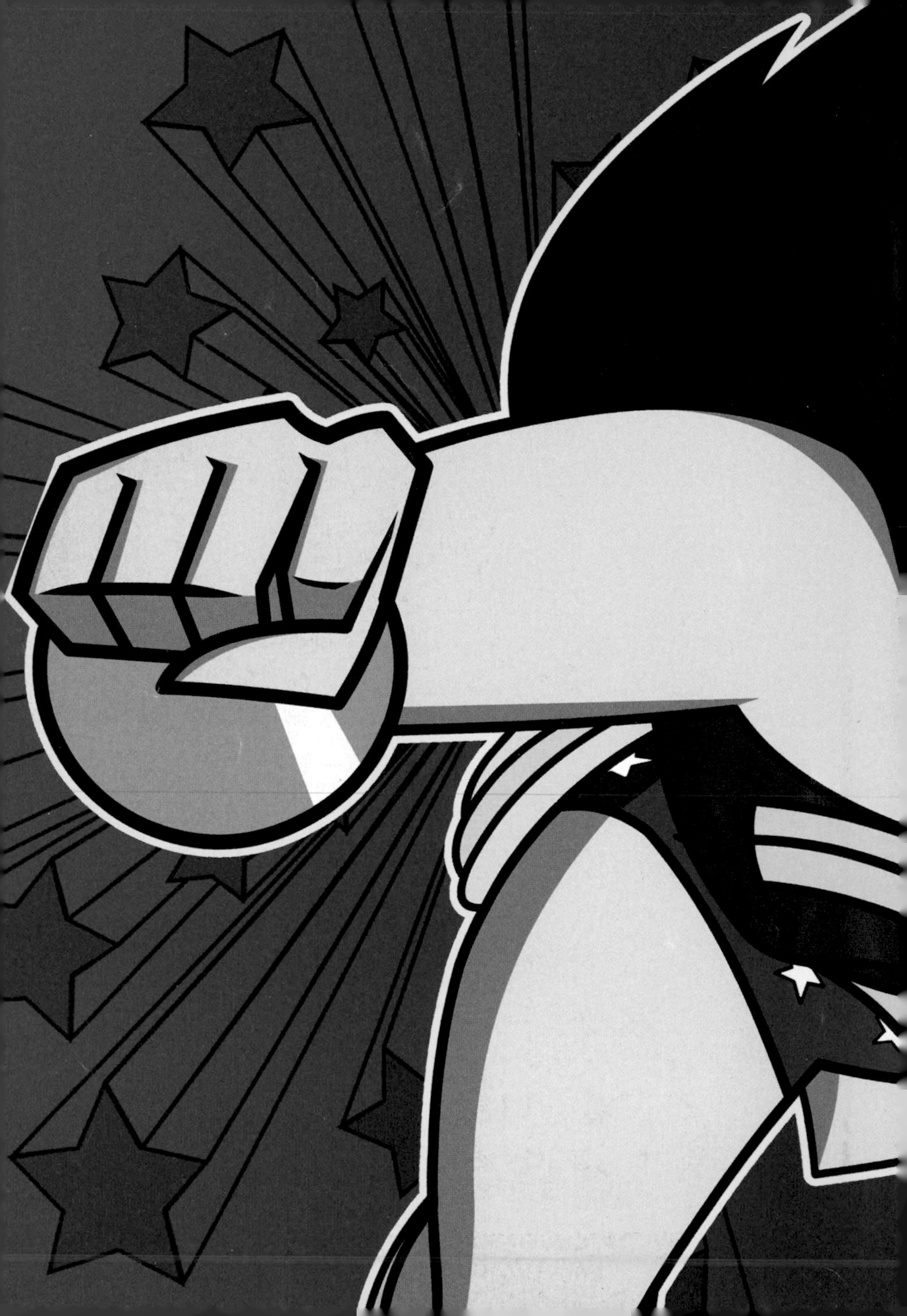